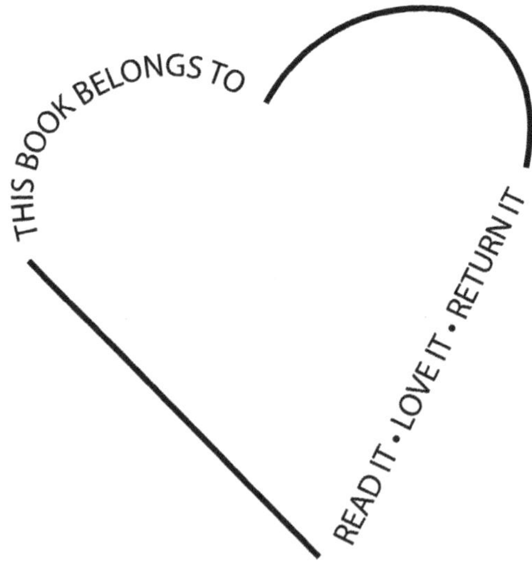
THIS BOOK BELONGS TO
READ IT • LOVE IT • RETURN IT

Dedication

To my handsome son, Mezziah, who is hands down the best brother ever! Life would be so colorless without you. To my loving husband, Joshua, who always encourages me to chase my dreams. You are my life partner. I love you forever! To my miracle daughter, Zyla, who purposefully brought me closer to GOD! You are the sunshine on all of my cloudy days.

And, this goes without saying, to my supporters. Thank you for picking up this book. Your support means more than you could ever imagine! Above all, to the siblings of the world: having a lifetime friend is priceless. Hug your brothers and sisters tightly. No relationship matters more than that of your sibling, I love you Pumpkin!

With a huge hug & a ton of kisses,
Cheleste P. Estrada

MY PARENTS ARE HAVING A BABY AND I KNOW I SHOULD BE HAPPY, BUT I AM EXTREMELY SAD. WHAT ABOUT MY MORNING HUGS AND KISSES FROM MOM, AND PLAYDATES WITH DAD?

MOM SAYS I WILL BE A BIG BROTHER, BUT WHAT DOES THAT REALLY MEAN?
WILL I HAVE TO SHARE MY TOYS? CHANGE DIAPERS? HELP CLEAN?

I JUST DON'T THINK I'M READY TO GIVE UP BEING AN ONLY CHILD.
WILL MY PARENTS STILL LOVE ME? WILL I STILL BE ENOUGH?
BEING AN OLDER BROTHER SOUNDS PRETTY TOUGH.

"HEY JACOB, WHY ARE YOU SO DOWN IN THE DUMPS? WOULD YOU LIKE TO TALK ABOUT IT IN THE KITCHEN WHILE I MAKE US SOME LUNCH?" MOM ASKS.

"MOM, I AM AFRAID THAT THINGS WILL CHANGE WHEN THE NEW BABY COMES.
WILL WE STILL GO FOR WALKS IN THE PARK AND RECITE THE ABCS, GO FOR VISITS TO THE ZOO,
WATCH MOVIES AND EAT MINT CHOCOLATE CHIP ICE CREAM?

I AM AFRAID THAT ONCE THE BABY COMES, YOU'LL FORGET ABOUT ME AND ALL THE FUN STUFF WE DO," EXPRESSES JACOB.

MOM REPLIED LOVINGLY, "I KNOW IT SEEMS SCARY AND IT'S SOMETHING NEW.
BUT, YOU ARE GOING TO BE THE BEST BIG BROTHER I PROMISE YOU.
YOU ARE OUR FIRST BORN CHILD AND THAT WILL NEVER CHANGE.
YOU CAN HELP PUT YOUR SISTER TO BED,
AND WE CAN SING LULLABIES LIKE TWINKLE TWINKLE LITTLE STAR.

DO YOU KNOW HOW LOVED YOU ARE?
WE WILL STILL GO FOR WALKS, BIKE RIDES IN THE PARK,
ICE CREAM DATES, AND MAKE STOPS AT THE ZOO."

"SHARING IS CARING AND SIBLINGS ARE FUN.
ALTHOUGH YOU DON'T THINK MUCH OF IT NOW,
THE BEST IS YET TO COME." MOM STATES.

"HEY SON, COME HELP ME BUILD YOUR SISTER'S CRIB," DAD EXCITEDLY SAYS.
JACOB REPLIES HESITANTLY, "REALLY, DAD? WHAT IF I DON'T DO A GOOD JOB?"
"I THINK YOU'LL DO GREAT! REMEMBER WHEN YOU HELPED ME BUILD YOUR TOY CHEST?"
JUICY

"YES, WE DID HAVE SO MUCH FUN. I REMEMBER DOING A JOB WELL DONE. BUILDING A CRIB SEEMS KIND OF TOUGH, BUT DOING OUR BEST SHOULD BE ENOUGH," JACOB SAYS PROUDLY.

"THAT'S THE SPIRIT! YOUR SISTER IS SO LUCKY TO HAVE YOU AS A BIG BROTHER!" DAD EXCLAIMS.

"HEY GUYS, JUNGLE ANIMALS OR UNICORNS? WHICH WILL BE MORE FUN?" MOM ASKS EXCITEDLY.

B C D E F G H

"JUNGLE ANIMALS! WE CAN PRETEND TO BE A LION AND TIGER ROARING IN THE HOT SUN," JACOB SAYS HAPPILY.

"Great choice, Jacob. She'll be here before we know it, and everything will be perfect," Mom says while hugging Jacob.

"WAHHHHH WAHHHH!!!" CRIES JACOB'S LITTLE SISTER.

"Being a big brother is special after all.
I promise to always be there to catch you when you fall.
Welcome baby sister, we are going to have a ball.

PS. IF YOUR CRIB FALLS APART, DAD BUILT IT, NOT ME."
Big Brother

THE END

www.ingramcontent.com/pod-product-compliance
Lightning Source LLC
LaVergne TN
LVHW070208110826
845147LV00002B/533

9780578242637